NORTH EAST of SCOTLAND LIBRARY SERVICE
14 Crown Terrace, Aberdeen

Thomas Edison

Josephine Ross

Illustrated by
Peter Gregory

Hamish Hamilton
London

Titles in the **Profiles** *series*

For my father

First published 1982 by
Hamish Hamilton Children's Books
Garden House, 57-59 Long Acre, London WC2E 9JZ
© text 1982 by Josephine Ross
© illustrations 1982 by Hamish Hamilton Ltd
Reprinted 1984
All rights reserved
ISBN 0-241-10713-X

Cover photograph reproduced by courtesy of
The Mansell Collection

Typeset by Pioneer
Printed in Great Britain at the
University Press, Cambridge

Contents

1   The 'Addled' Boy

On a December night in 1877, the workers at the Menlo Park laboratory, in New Jersey, USA, gathered to watch the first trial of a strange-looking new machine. As they waited expectantly, the inventor Thomas Edison turned a handle on the machine and in a loud, high voice, said the words, 'Mary had a little lamb'. A few moments later he turned the handle again — and to everybody's astonishment his voice, saying the nursery rhyme, could be clearly heard, coming out of the machine.

'I was never so taken aback in my life', Edison said afterwards. It was a historic moment. Man had recorded sound, for the first time; and this 'phonograph', the earliest gramophone, was one of the great discoveries for which Thomas Alva Edison was to become famous throughout the world, as 'The man who invented the future'.

When Edison was born, on 11 February 1847, not only were there no gramophones or records in people's lives, there were no telephones, no films and no electric lights either. In the United States of America, where his parents had recently settled, slaves still worked on the old plantations of the deep South, and tribes of Indians, such as the legendary Sioux and Cheyenne, roamed the prairies of the West. Among Edison's earliest memories was the sight of pioneer families setting out in covered wagons for the gold-fields of California; and the first railroad, the 'Iron Horse', which was to play such an important part in Thomas Alva Edison's young life, did not reach his neighbourhood until he was seven years old.

Milan, Ohio, where he was born, was then a small, peaceful town in the mid-West. The Edison family had first come to America from their native Holland during the 1730s; later they moved to Canada, and it was only ten years before the birth of Thomas Edison that his parents, Samuel and Nancy, returned to the United States and settled in Milan. There they lived simply but comfortably, in a sloping brick and stone house which can still be seen today. Samuel started a small timber business, and Nancy bore three more children. They named the youngest Thomas, after an ancestor, and Alva, after a family friend, but he soon became known to everyone as just 'Al'.

From his earliest years, Al Edison showed a spirit of adventure. Some of the wilder stories which were told about his boyhood were almost certainly made up after he became famous; as an adult he himself often gave exaggerated accounts of his life in newspaper interviews. But there is no doubt that he was a lively boy with an enquiring mind, and whether or not he actually set fire to a barn, fell into a canal and was publicly beaten by his father in the town square, as people later claimed, Al Edison was certainly not a model child.

Edison's birthplace in Milan, Ohio

He did not even do well at school. After his family moved in 1854 to Port Huron, Michigan, 160 kilometres north of Milan, Al became very ill with scarlet fever, so it was not until the following year, when he was eight years old, that he became a pupil at the local school. He stayed there for only three unhappy months, however. One day he came home looking very upset, and told his mother that the teacher had called him 'addled' — meaning he was backward. Nancy Edison, who had once been a teacher herself, was furious. She marched off to the school, taking Al with her, and told the schoolmaster he didn't know what he was talking about. In future, she announced, she would give Al his lessons herself, at home. Edison never forgot that scene. 'She was the most enthusiastic champion a boy ever had', he recalled later. 'I determined right then that I would be worthy of her.'

From that day on, Al learned fast. Instead of forcing him to remember long lists of dull facts, as the unsympathetic schoolmaster had done, Nancy Edison encouraged her son to read, to follow his interests, and to think for himself. Her teaching method had its drawbacks — until he was grown up, Al had no idea of spelling or grammar, and he disliked mathematics all his life. But he loved reading, often choosing books far in advance of his age, and anything to do with science — particularly chemistry — fascinated him.

'His early amusements were steam engines and mechanical forces', his father once said. A corner of the cellar in the Edisons' home became Al's private laboratory, and there, using old bottles and chemicals bought with his pocket-money, he carried out his own experiments. While other boys were playing games outside, or fishing, Al was down in the cellar with his science text-books, mixing up chemicals. Bangs, smells and upsets sometimes resulted when experiments went wrong, but if Nancy Edison was occasionally annoyed by the mess Al made, she was immensely proud of her lively, clever son.

One recent invention which particularly captured Al's interest was the telegraph. In the 1850s telephones were still unknown, but the first mechanical method by which man could communicate over long distances had

Edison's parents, Samuel and Nancy

been developed. It was given the name of telegraphy. Using the Morse Code — the system of dots and dashes representing the alphabet, which Samuel Morse had invented — trained operators could send messages across hundreds of kilometres, by means of electrical charges in telegraph wires. Al taught himself the Morse Code and set up his own home-made telegraph wire between his house and a friend's. 'It worked fine', he remembered years later with satisfaction.

The coming of the railroad to Port Huron, in 1859, was the most important event in Edison's young life. Like the telegraph, the steam-engine seemed a marvel of modern science in those days, and to the mechanically-minded Al it must have been especially fascinating. But unlike most twelve-year-old boys, he was not limited merely to reading and dreaming about trains — with his father's encouragement, he applied for a job on the railroads.

9

Samuel Edison had never been a rich man, and as Al grew older money had become scarce in the Edison household. The boy's earnings as a newsboy with the Grand Trunk Railroad would be useful. In winning over his mother to the scheme, Al had to use great persistence. Four of the Edison children had died young, leaving Al the youngest of the family by fourteen years; Nancy was not happy at the prospect of letting her last and cleverest child go off to work at the age of twelve. But she was won over in the end, and the 'addled' boy, who was to grow up to become one of America's greatest inventors, set out on the first stage of his career.

2 On The Railroad

Every morning at 7 a.m. the great iron engine steamed out of the station at Port Huron, and set off down the tracks for the 100-kilometre journey to Detroit. There were goods in the wagons and passengers in the carriages — and during the four-hour ride the newsboy darted up and down the crowded cars, offering his newspapers and refreshments to the travellers.

It was a long, hard day's work for a boy of Al's age. On arriving at Detroit the train halted for a lengthy 'stopover', and it was not until 9.30 in the evening, 14½ hours after he had set out, that Al reached Port Huron again. Yet he seems to have enjoyed the busy life of the railroad, with its promise of travel and excitement, and, as always, he made the most of his opportunities.

During the stopovers in Detroit he headed for the local library, and there spent his free hours, eagerly reading. 'I didn't read a few books, I read the library', he once said. Some of the works he chose, such as Isaac Newton's *Principia*, were heavy reading for a youngster, but thanks to Nancy's early teaching, Al's eagerness to learn made almost any book seem exciting.

In spite of his literary tastes, young Edison was far from being a priggish bookworm. 'Cheeky' was how he

Edison at the age of fourteen

described himself, and a photograph taken when he was fourteen shows him as a merry-looking youngster with shabby clothes and a big grin. His liking for books was more than equalled by his mischievous sense of adventure — and a good deal of his energy went into finding ways of making money.

Because he was not paid wages by the railroad company, but made his earnings from what he sold on the trains, Al was always looking for ways to increase his profits. As well as newspapers and sweets, he began to sell local produce from Port Huron, such as butter and fruit in season. His parents' garden provided him with fresh vegetables to sell to housewives on the morning run. Before long he had other boys working for him, and his business showed a small but pleasing profit.

The men who worked on the trains, and the telegraph operators who were based at the railway stations, seem to have liked the energetic young newsboy. They were 'a good-natured lot of men and kind to me', Edison said in later years. One of the trainmen allowed him to set up a laboratory in a corner of a baggage compartment, where he could keep his precious chemicals and carry on with his experiments. The telegraph operators must have got to know him well, as he hung around their machines and watched them tap out information from station to station in their rapid Morse Code. It became one of Al's greatest ambitions that one day he, too, would be a telegraphist, and send out messages across the wires.

Among the legacies of Edison's years on the railroads there was one lasting sorrow: he went very deaf. How it happened is still something of a mystery. His childhood attack of scarlet fever was the most likely cause, though a blow to the head, such as a box on the ears, could also have done the damage. Edison's own explanation of how it started is dramatic, but unlikely, according to modern doctors. He claimed, years later, that he had been trying to board a moving train with his arms full of newspapers; as he reached the rear step, a helpful guard leaned out, grasped him by the ears and hauled him up.

'I felt something snap inside my head', Edison recounted, 'and the deafness started from that time and has progressed ever since.' He never became stone deaf, but some sounds were lost to him for ever, and others grew very faint. 'I haven't heard a bird sing since I was twelve years old', he once wrote sadly. Edison's lack of hearing often made him feel very isolated, and taking part in conversations became increasingly difficult for him in adult life. Yet, like many people with a handicap, he made the best of it — and even managed to turn it to his advantage at times. When in later years he was developing the telephone and inventing the gramophone, his own difficulty in hearing made him insist that the machines must produce the clearest possible sound. He also had the deaf person's liking for his own company, and unusual powers of concentration. In spite of — or perhaps partly because of — his deafness, Al Edison was determined to get on in the world.

His quick wits were sharpened by his experiences on the railroad. He learned a great deal about human nature, and this, too, he turned to his advantage. Having discovered that sensational stories in the newspapers always increased his sales, he got into the habit of finding out in advance what the headline news was to be, so that he could judge how many copies to take onto the train with him. On one famous occasion this brought him a windfall. The American Civil War, between the Union army of the north and the Confederates in the south, had broken out in 1861, when Al was fourteen. The first major battle was fought at Shiloh, in May 1862, with huge casualties; here, Al realised, was the newspaper report the public would be clamouring to read! With a stroke of inspiration, he asked the telegraph operators all down the line to contact the stations, and have the news of the battle chalked up on the boards usually reserved for train information. Crowds gathered at every stop, frantic to 'read all about it' in the newspapers — and even thought he raised his prices that day, Al could have sold all his extra copies many times over.

Earlier that year, not content with merely selling newspapers, Al had decided to start one of his own. The result was *The Weekly Herald* — probably the only newspaper ever produced in the baggage wagon of a train, by a proprietor in his early teens. It carried local news, advertisements, announcements of births, marriages and deaths among the railroad employees, and a few jokes for good measure. The circulation was naturally limited, as was the young owner's knowledge of spelling, but it was an impressive achievement for a boy of Al's age. For all the hardships of those years on the railroads, they were a valuable preparation for what lay ahead.

3   The Young Telegraphist

Any thoughts Thomas Edison might have had of becoming a real journalist, and spending his working life in newspaper offices, came to an end in the summer of 1862, just a few months after the Battle of Shiloh. An act of bravery, performed almost without thinking, brought him an unexpected reward, and set him on the path that was to lead to a brilliant future.

He was standing in the station at Mount Clemens, waiting while the train shunted a heavy boxcar out of a siding. As he watched, the wagon began to roll down the line — and to his horror, he suddenly noticed that the telegraph operator's baby son had wandered onto the tracks, and was playing there happily, unaware of any danger. Without hesitating, Al flung himself towards the child, scooped him up, and ran with him to safety, just in time.

Al Edison became the hero of Mount Clemens. The father of the child he had just rescued, a Scotsman named Mr Mackenzie, knew just how to thank him; he offered to teach him all about telegraphy. Overjoyed, Al accepted.

During the weeks that followed, Al learned the mysteries of professional telegraph operating, until he was as expert as Mr Mackenzie himself. At the age of sixteen, the former newsboy was ready for his first job as a junior, 'plug', operator.

His chance to break into telegraphy had come at a good moment. The American Civil War had created a vast demand for telegraph operators, both within the armies, to operate military communications, and in civilian life, to send press reports and keep the anxious public supplied with up-to-date information on battles, casualties and the progress of the war. As it happened, the little telegraph office in Port Huron was looking for a new telegraphist, to replace one who had gone off to work for the army. Al Edison, the bright local boy, was

Edison's stock-ticker. This machine relayed the latest Stock Exchange prices to businessmen's offices

the obvious choice for the job — and he got it. That was the beginning of six eventful years, in which he moved about from place to place, and from job to job, as a 'tramp' telegraphist.

It turned out that Al was not by any means the ideal employee, in spite of his skills. Though he learned fast, and developed a unique telegraphic style of his own that was, in the words of a colleague, 'detected by its lightning-like rapidity', his mind was not always on his work. When possible, he chose to work night shifts, so that his days would be left free for private study and experiments; the result was that he was often tired and slapdash when it came to doing his job. While he was employed as a Station Operator at Stratford Junction, across the border in Canada, he devised a scheme which would allow him to catch up on his sleep during working hours. The telegraph operator was supposed to send a signal out to the central control office at regular intervals, to show that he was awake and concentrating. Edison invented a clockwork device that would send his signal automatically, while he had some much-needed rest. Needless to say, his superiors were not impressed by that particular invention when it was discovered, and it was not long before Edison was on the move once more.

From Ontario back to Michigan, from Indianapolis to the big city of Cincinnati, he roved about the American mid-West, staying in cheap lodgings, sleeping little, studying hard and spending more of his wages than he could afford on books and equipment. And all the time, ideas and inventions kept coming into his busy mind.

18

Throughout his career, Edison showed a talent for seeing a need and then finding an ingenious way to answer it. As a young telegraphist he began by inventing devices that would make his work easier — such as a simple Morse repeater, by which a message delivered at great speed could be re-run by the operator on the receiving end, just as fast or as slowly as suited him.

Clearly, there were commercial possibilities for Al's ideas. In 1868, with hopes of finding a market in the big city, perhaps even making his fortune, he decided to head for Boston. He was a tobacco-chewing country boy with rough clothes and a broad mid-western accent, but his talent counted for more than his appearance, and the powerful Western Union Telegraph company took him on as a night operator in their big Boston office. Working by nights, studying and inventing by day, it was not long before he had produced his first real commercial invention. It was an automatic device for recording representatives' votes in Congress — the American Parliament. For this, he applied for a 'patent', the legal registration of an idea which would prevent anyone else from copying it. Edison's automatic vote recorder was a simple, ingenious, potentially useful idea — and it was a total failure. No-one wanted it.

Young Edison was not to be put off by failure, however. In December 1868 he took the bold step of resigning from Western Union, and setting out to work as an independent inventor. He was now working on two main projects — a 'duplex' telegraph system, by which two messages could be sent at once over the same telegraph machine, and a mechanical stock-ticker. The stock-ticker offered a valuable service to businessmen, by relaying to their offices the latest news of the constantly-changing Stock Exchange prices. Though Edison was not the first person to produce either duplex telegraphy or a stock-ticker, his versions vastly improved and extended the previous systems. But again he met with disappointment. He had a limited success with his stock-ticker, but neither of the big telegraph companies in Boston would back his duplex telegraph operations. There was nothing else for it — he would go to New York, and try his luck there.

4   The Invention Factory

Shabby, penniless and desperate to find work, Edison arrived in New York in the early summer of 1869, aged twenty-two. He had nowhere to stay and no immediate job prospects; when he approached Western Union, he was told they could offer him nothing. It was one of the darkest moments of his career.

His most urgent need was for a place to stay — and in this Edison had an unexpected stroke of luck. He called on the Laws Gold Indicator Company, only to learn that there was no job going; however, the chief engineer there, Franklin Pope, had heard of Edison's talents, and felt he deserved encouragement. He told the young inventor that he could use the office as his base, and sleep there until he found lodgings.

It was a chance, and Edison always made the most of his chances. He now set about finding out all he could about the workings of the company which was his temporary home.

As he already knew, gold-dealing had risen to fever pitch after the Civil War. To keep dealers up to date with the rapidly-changing gold prices, the Vice President of the New York Gold Exchange, Dr Samuel Laws, had invented an automatic machine which

Edison (in middle age) operating a telegraph

displayed the current prices at the Exchange. Laws then developed a system for transmitting the information shown on this indicator into dealers' own offices, all over the city. His inventions proved so successful that he retired from his position with the Gold Exchange, and set up the Laws Gold Indicator Company.

Roaming freely about the Laws offices, studying the equipment with his expert eye, Edison soon made himself familiar with the way the machinery worked.

And so it happened that when a crisis suddenly occurred, and one of the parts of a transmitter broke down, it was Edison who spotted the fault, and was able to put it right. Dr Laws was surprised and delighted; he promptly offered this remarkable young stranger a job as assistant to Franklin Pope. And when Pope left the firm soon after, Edison replaced him, at a salary of 300 dollars a month.

To the poor country boy newly arrived in the big city, it must have felt like something out of a fairy tale. At last he had been given the chance to show what he could do — and he was being paid what seemed to him a small fortune to do so! During that summer he worked away, adapting, designing, inventing, and produced — among other things — an improved version of his own stock-ticker, and a better gold-indicator.

The next step was still more exciting. Edison decided to leave the Laws company, and set up in business for himself, with Pope, who had remained his friend, and a publisher named Ashley. A notice in the press announced that Pope, Edison and Company, Electrical Engineers and General Telegraphic Agency, could offer a wide range of services, from designing special telegraphic equipment to suit clients' needs, to producing fire and burglar alarms. What they were selling, above all, was Edison's remarkable ability to recognise a mechanical need or problem, and devise a brilliant solution to it.

The powerful Western Union Company began to show a new interest in this former employee whose services they had turned down not long before. When Edison

23

Edison's first wife, Mary

came up with a clever new system for transmitting gold prices, which he called his 'gold printer', Western Union bought up the rights, for 15,000 dollars. Even when this

24

sum was split with his two partners, it seemed a huge amount to Edison, and he was able to write home proudly, 'Don't do any hard work and get mother anything she desires. You can draw on me for money.' He signed this letter 'Thomas A'. It seemed more suitable for a successful New York businessman than plain 'Al'.

General Lefferts, an important executive of the Western Union's Gold and Stock Telegraph division, kept Edison well supplied with orders — and before long the young inventor decided to break away from his partners altogether, and set up on his own. It was thanks largely to Lefferts that Thomas Edison was able, at the age of twenty-four, to turn his dream of starting his own 'invention factory' into reality.

What happened was that Edison produced an exceptionally important invention, which made it possible for breakdowns of individual stock-printers to be corrected automatically, from central office, instead of by the laborious process of sending out an engineer to dismantle the machine. Seeing the potential of this discovery, General Lefferts sent for Edison and announced that he would like to buy the rights; how much did the inventor want for them?

Edison hesitated, wondering if he dared ask as much as 5,000 dollars. Before he could reply, Lefferts suggested a price — 40,000 dollars! Thomas Edison very nearly fainted. Then, recovering, he just managed to say that he thought it was a fair offer.

In fact, it was a fortune to him. He knew so little about money at that time that he even had difficulty in understanding how a bank account worked. But he joyfully described himself as 'a bloated Eastern manufacturer' in a letter to his parents, and he lost no time in putting his new wealth to work for him. He was going to start his own business, manufacturing his inventions — beginning with a large order for his stock-tickers for Western Union.

During the winter of 1871 he searched for premises, until he found what he wanted, at 4-6 Ward Street, Newark, New Jersey, and then he began stocking them with equipment. He spent his money freely in the process; to Edison, the whole point of having wealth was to expand his inventing operations. Ever since his early days as a newsboy he had been good at finding ways of making money, but managing it was not one of his strong points. Book-keeping, like mathematics, bored him, and his bills were rarely paid on time. Everything in Edison's life — even eating, sleeping and dressing — had to take second place to his all-important work.

In many ways, Edison was like the popular idea of a typical inventor, right down to his unusual clothes and appearance. His face was interesting and attractive, with large eyes and a broad forehead under a mop of unruly hair; at a time when most men wore whiskers and beards he was always clean-shaven, which accentuated his strong features. There was no mistaking the country cut of his clothes when he first arrived in New York, and one of the Newark employees thought he dressed like a tramp. But even after success and wealth had come his way, when he travelled the world and dined with

Presidents, he seemed to pay little attention to how he looked.

The group of talented co-workers whom Edison gathered around him at the Newark factory learned to tolerate their employer's odd ways. One of them later recalled how excited he used to become; when his work was going badly he would 'swear something awful', but

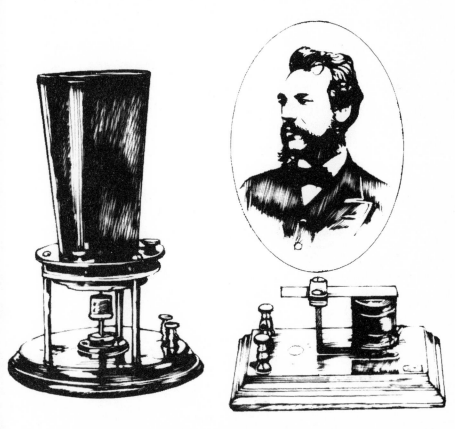

Alexander Graham Bell with his invention, the first telephone.
On the left is the transmitter, on the right, the receiver

when an invention was finished he would 'jump up and do a kind of Zulu war-dance' for joy. Though the men had to work long hours, they knew that Edison was working even harder — and his enthusiasm was infectious. Life in the invention factory might be demanding, but it was certainly never dull.

The five years which Edison spent at Newark were among the happiest of his life. During this period, he produced a series of important inventions, including the first really successful automatic telegraph, as well as the new 'diplex' telegraph, by which two messages could be sent at once, in the same direction, from the same machine, and the 'quadruplex' telegraph, which allowed four separate messages, passing in opposite directions, to be sent out from two separate machines at once.

In spite of his constant preoccupation with his work, Thomas Edison found time to fall in love and get married, less than a year after setting up the invention factory. His bride was a pretty blonde sixteen-year-old named Mary Stilwell; when they married, on Christmas Day 1871, the couple were clearly very much in love. The new Mrs Edison was sweet-natured and submissive, with little claim to intellect, and she seems to have fitted in uncomplainingly with the nineteenth-century role of housewife and mother, devoting herself to making a comfortable home for her brilliant husband. In the Edison household, 'Father's work always came first'.

5   Edison And The Telephone

As a family joke, Edison's elder daughter and son —
Marion and Thomas — were nicknamed 'Dot' and
'Dash', after the Morse Code telegraphic symbols. The
telegraph had been the basis of all his important
inventions so far — but in 1875 a new scientific marvel
was being developed which was to take Edison's talents
in a different direction.

He had already done some experimenting with sound
waves when, early in 1876, a young Scots immigrant
named Alexander Graham Bell applied for a patent for
a device which would transform the vibrations from
sound waves into electric current. This amazing
discovery was to provide the basis of the modern
telephone. Bell invented it; Edison developed it.

The telegraph companies, having at first dismissed
the new discovery as unimportant, began to regard it as
a threat to their own services. The President of Western
Union, William Orton, decided to take action; he
commissioned Edison to produce another version of the
telephone, that would be more commercial than Bell's.
With his usual single-minded dedication, Edison set to
work in the autumn of 1876.

'I am having pretty hard luck with my speaking

telegraph, but I think it is OK now', he wrote to his father, as the work progressed. There were several ways in which he believed he could improve upon Bell's original 'magnetotelephone'. With Bell's machine, it was the vibrations made by the human voice, inducing electrical impulses, that caused the spoken words to be reproduced at the other end of the line. The sounds thus produced were very faint, and became even fainter over long distances. Edison chose to employ a different method. On his machine, the voice caused a valve to open or close, and this regulated the necessary current, allowing for much better reproduction of sounds. With his own difficulty in hearing, Edison was determined that his telephone should offer the clearest possible sound.

His greatest contribution to the telephone was the invention of the 'carbon button transmitter' which, in its modern form, is still used today. On Bell's machine, the same instrument had to act as both receiver and transmitter, but Edison separated these, so that, as now, the user would speak into one part and listen to another. Through months of research and experiment, he discovered that the best substance to use for sound reproduction inside the transmitter was a plug of carbon. In his words, this 'gave splendid results, the articulation being distinct and the volume of sound several times greater than with telephones worked on the magneto principle'.

William Orton was impressed with Edison's results; he paid the enormous sum of 100,000 dollars for the rights to the carbon transmitter. Western Union founded

Menlo Park laboratory

the American Speaking Telephone Company, to compete with Bell and his backers, and from then on a bitter commercial rivalry was under way. The result was a tangle of legal battles over rights and patents. Edison himself summed up the situation with the dry comment that the Western Union was pirating the Bell receiver, and Bell's company was pirating the Western Union transmitter.

In the autumn of 1878 the miracle of the telephone — and also the accompanying legal battles — came to Britain, amid much publicity. Edison's representatives in England arranged for public tests of their telephone to be carried out, and these were a great success. However, before they could win the hoped-for Post Office contract to set up a telephone network across Britain, a new law-suit loomed. Though the transmitter used in the tests was Edison's, the receiver was the one invented by Bell, which had already been patented in London. The Bell company threatened to sue if this continued; it seemed a major setback.

For Edison, however, it was simply a new challenge. 'In Britain we had fun', he remarked mischievously, years later. As usual, he was able to find a solution to the problem. Bell's 'magnetotelephone' used a magnet in the receiver; after a period of intensive work, Edison came up with a receiver which had no magnet, but instead contained a chalk cylinder. The result was the 'loud-speaking telephone', which had an even clearer tone than the previous version.

Some hearers felt it was rather too clear. Then, as now, there were complaints that the telephone was more of a nuisance than a blessing, and that it intruded on people's lives. But others were impressed, including the Prince of Wales (the future King Edward VII) and the Prime Minister, Mr Gladstone, both of whom attended a demonstration and tried out Edison's telephone for themselves, on 15 March 1879. The telephone had come to stay.

The competition between the Bell and Edison companies in Britain was brought to its obvious conclusion when, in June 1880, the two firms joined forces, to form the United Telephone Company. For Edison himself it was a highly satisfactory outcome; he received an enormous sum for his rights, and he was now free to concentrate on his other inventions. While the disputes over the telephone were going on, he had been busy with some of the most important work of his life.

6   Genius At Work

During the early stages of his work on the telephone, a major change had taken place in Edison's life: he had left Newark and moved, with his family and team of workers, to the little hamlet of Menlo Park. Set in the countryside of New Jersey, 40 kilometres outside New York, Menlo Park provided the ideal setting for his new laboratory — peaceful and secluded, yet easily reached by the increasing numbers of journalists and visitors who were eager to see the great man at work. Like Shakespeare's Stratford-upon-Avon, or the Prince Regent's Brighton, the name of Menlo Park was to become permanently associated with that of its most famous resident, Thomas Alva Edison.

The great move took place in 1876. The Edisons and their children moved into a large, pleasant house, conveniently close to the laboratory and workshops which were being specially built to Edison's requirements. In this setting, he was to spend the next ten years of his working life — and it was here at Menlo Park that two of the most important inventions of recent times came into being.

People, as well as ideas, flourished at Menlo Park. The atmosphere in the laboratory was happy and

Edison (seated) with Charles Batchelor, his engineer

unconventional; Edison's small daughter sometimes played on the floor beside him as he worked, and there was a great deal of joking and teasing. Edison prided himself on being able to send an audience into fits of laughter with his funny stories. Visitors often went away singing — leaving the inventor and his team, having finished their supper, to return to their desks and benches, where they would work until far into the night. Like many great men of history, Edison himself would snatch his sleep when and where he could, often catnapping, fully-clothed, with his head resting on a scientific manual.

The family feeling that existed at Menlo Park was partly due to the fact that most of the leading members of the Newark team had moved there with Edison. Among them was an English-born engineer named Charles Batchelor, and a Swiss watch-maker, John Kreusi, both of whom were to become famous. Later on, as the little community expanded, other workers with specialist skills joined the group — even, in 1878, a brilliant mathematician, called Francis Upton, who supplied the mathematical knowledge which Edison himself lacked. Edison asked a great deal of these 'friends and co-workers', as he described them, but they willingly gave up free time and private life to work in a happy environment with a man they liked and admired, on tasks that were always challenging. It said a good deal for Edison's personality that he could inspire such dedication in the group of people who worked with him day and night.

There was certainly no lack of variety in their lives. Edison had the remarkable ability of being able to work on several different projects at once, turning from one to another as the mood took him. He filled hundreds of notebooks with plans and sketches, sometimes breaking off in the middle of eating or talking to jot down an idea which had occurred to him. A minor invention every ten days and an important one every six months was his stated production target for the Menlo Park laboratory. And if he made that remark with his tongue in his cheek, the fact remains that a steady stream of inventions came out of Menlo Park.

All these inventions were designed to fulfil some strictly practical need — usually, in the early years, connected with telegraphy. Scientific discovery for its own sake had no place in Edison's life: he was only interested in producing machines and devices which would have a commercial use. As in the case of the telephone, he often worked to order, finding a way to meet a client's special need. The more difficult the task, the more he seemed to enjoy the challenge.

It was Edison who coined the famous phrase, 'Genius is one percent inspiration and ninety-nine percent perspiration', during a newspaper interview. Out at Menlo Park, home of the telephone transmitter, the phonograph and the electric light, genius was hard at work.

7   The First Phonograph

Among all Edison's marvellous inventions, one in particular stands out as his 'greatest single achievement' — the phonograph, or the original gramophone. Much of his life's work involved developing and improving devices for which the basis already existed, as in the case of the telephone and, later, the incandescent light bulb; but the machine which would record and reproduce sound, which he first gave to the world, was entirely the result of his own original thought and research.

Since photography had been discovered, early in the 19th century, there had been speculation that it might be possible to reproduce sound, as well as visual images. No-one had discovered how it could be done, however. Then, almost by accident, Thomas Edison became interested in the idea — and by the summer of 1877 he was involved in the task of finding a way to 'store up and reproduce automatically' the sound of human speech.

Because of his own troublesome deafness, and also because of his close involvement with the development of the telephone, he had a special interest in the subject of sound. While he was working on the telephone, he had observed the effect which the human voice had on a diaphragm, making it vibrate strongly. Then another of

The first phonograph

his projects, for an automatic telegraph repeater which would record telegraphic signals, gave him the vital clue as to how speech might be recorded.

This telegraph repeater was a remarkable machine which could print an incoming Morse Code message in tiny raised dots and dashes on a strip of waxed paper. While trying out the machine, Edison had an idea: if a series of indentations on paper could be made to reproduce the click of a telegraph, could not the vibrations of a diaphragm be recorded and reproduced also? It was an exciting thought, and he pursued it.

He proceeded to rig up a makeshift instrument, using a diaphragm with a blunt pin attached to it, and a strip of paraffined paper. Watched by his disbelieving co-worker, Charles Batchelor, Edison pulled the strip of paper through the machine and shouted, 'Hulloo!' into it. Then the paper was pulled through again — and the two men, 'listening breathlessly', heard a distinct sound, faintly resembling the word 'Hulloo'. It was all the encouragement Edison needed to go on with the work, even though Batchelor bet him a barrel of apples that he would never make a success of it.

Though Edison continued to work on other projects, the talking machine gradually took shape during the summer and autumn of 1877. Newspaper articles revealed that Mr Edison was planning an important new device, similar to his telegraph recorder, that would act as a telephone repeater and be able to record and re-transmit whatever was said over the telephone. No-one at that stage, not even the inventor himself, seemed to realise the full importance of what was happening at Menlo Park.

References and sketches among Edison's notes show the progress of the new machine, which was christened the 'phonograph', from the Greek words 'phono', meaning 'sound', and 'graph', 'writing'. Even when the plans were ready, at the beginning of December, and John Kreusi was handed the instructions from which he was to make up the first phonograph, Edison admitted that he didn't have much faith that it would work. When the purpose of the machine was explained to Kreusi, he said frankly he thought it was absurd. It was a sceptical group of laboratory workers who gathered, on the night of 4 December 1877, to see the machine tried out for the first time.

The original strip of waxed paper had been done away with; and in its place the stylus now indented its

Edison, exhausted after staying up all night to test his phonograph

tiny marks onto a sheet of tinfoil wrapped around a cylinder with a deep groove in it. When a handle was turned, this cylinder rotated and moved along a screwed shaft. As Edison turned the handle, he spoke the childish words that were to go down in history, 'Mary had a little lamb'. He then took the needle off the recording diaphragm, returned the cylinder to its starting position, and brought the needle of the other diaphragm to rest on the tinfoil. Again he turned the handle; again his voice was heard saying 'Mary had a little lamb'; but this time, the inventor had not spoken. The machine had recorded his words, and played them back. Edison had invented the phonograph.

For those present, it was an unforgettable moment. They spent the rest of that night excitedly trying out the machine, talking into it, making noises, and playing back the sounds. During the days that followed they worked on alterations and improvements to the design, until it was ready to be patented. In the meantime, Edison announced his new invention to the world. Almost overnight, he became a celebrity. Newspapers and magazines devoted whole columns to the miraculous talking machine and its inventor, who became known as 'The Wizard of Menlo Park'. The editor of one publication, the *Scientific American*, reported that Mr Edison had brought the phonograph into his office, 'turned a crank, and the machine enquired as to our health, asked how we liked the phonograph, informed us that it was very well, and bid us a cordial good-night'. Soon everyone was clamouring to see the wonder for themselves. Visitors of all ages and nationalities

Phonograph cylinders

streamed into the little hamlet of Menlo Park, to look round the now-famous laboratory, hear the miraculous machine, and meet the friendly, tousle-haired thirty-year-old 'Wizard', who had given America and the world this marvel.

Edison thoroughly enjoyed all the attention. The former newsboy loved appearing in the papers, and he was always ready to provide journalists with a good snappy quotation, or a lively account of his doings. There was a good deal of the showman in him; he had always had a talent for acting and joke-telling, and he made the most of it when he demonstrated the phonograph. He would sing into it, chat to it, recite poetry or drama; and all these sounds, as well as coughs, cries and sneezes, the machine would play back quite clearly, to the delight of the audience. Among the many appreciative listeners was the then President of the United States, President Hayes, to whom Edison demonstrated the machine in April 1878, in the historic surroundings of the White House. The 'addled boy' had come a long way since his early years in Michigan.

Apart from the obvious entertainment value of the phonograph, Edison foresaw more serious uses for his invention. With improvements, not only could it record music, and entire books, which would be invaluable both in education and in providing 'talking books' for the blind, it could also be highly important in the business world, as a form of 'dictaphone', which he believed might eventually replace letter-writing and do away altogether with the need for secretaries and clerks. The businessman in Edison was always very much to

The Idelia (left) and Opera phonographs

the fore.

At thirty, Edison found himself hailed as a wizard, a genius, and one of America's great sons; the phonograph had made his name. 'I've made a good many machines', he told a journalist, 'but this is my baby, and I expect it to grow up to be a big feller, and support me in my old age'. Yet it was not in his nature to sit back and contemplate his success — and in 1878 one of his life's greatest achievements was still to come.

8 'The Light of The Future'

Much as Edison enjoyed the limelight, the ceaseless glare of publicity which followed his invention of the phonograph left him feeling tired and in need of a change. He went off on a working holiday, with a group of scientists; by the time he returned, in the autumn of 1878, he was ready to tackle a new and important project, which had long been in his mind. He was going to light up the world, by a 'safe, mild and inexpensive' new method of illumination, that would replace gas and oil lamps in people's lives.

There was nothing new in the idea of electric lighting. As long ago as 1810, the scientist Sir Humphrey Davy had demonstrated the carbon arc to the Royal Institution in London, showing how an arc of electric light could be made to jump between two carbon rods, or 'electrodes', each connected to a source of current. Other scientists and inventors carried on the work as the century progressed, and at different times streets and public places in London, Paris and St Petersburg were lit by improved forms of electric arc lighting. But this system, with its harsh glare, chemical smell, and need for constant attention, was not practical for general use. Edison, as his notes reveal, was interested in the

Edison with his dictaphone

possibilities of the carbon arc — but it was another method of lighting, the incandescent lamp, on which he chose to concentrate his attention.

As earlier inventors in this field had found, a filament of carbon sealed in an airless glass container would heat up and give off light if an electric current was passed through it. A young British chemist named Joseph Swan spent many years trying to find a way to put this principle into practice, and by the late 1870s he was close to success.

Meanwhile, on the other side of the Atlantic Ocean, Edison and the Menlo Park team were hard at work on their version of the electric light bulb. There were endless problems to be solved, from discovering the best material to use for the filament inside the glass bulb, to obtaining the large sums of money that would be needed to finance the research. But, as usual, Edison was able to find the answers.

With the support of powerful backers the Edison Electric Light Company was set up. As events were to show, it was important that the business side of the new invention should have been so well taken care of — even if, at the time when the company was formed, the invention itself scarcely existed.

Although recent developments in the world of science — such as the invention of the dynamo, to provide power, and the discovery of new ways of creating a vacuum — had done a great deal to make the invention of an incandescent light bulb possible, there was still a long way to go, as Edison (and his rivals) found. It was Edison who came up with such novel suggestions as the use of large, central power stations, 'piped' electricity supplies to people's homes, and even electricity meters. And after long months of trial and error, he eventually produced the filament of carbonised thread that would glow brightly for many hours, in a vacuum within a glass bulb. Even the shape of this early light bulb had to be patiently worked out, before the Menlo Park glassblowing expert, Ludwig Boehm, could apply his skills to making it.

Such was the confidence of Edison and his backers, however, that they kept the newspapers informed about the progress of the 'Wizard's' new marvel, from its earliest stages. The enthusiasm of the journalists and the interest of their readers was so great that the press reports sometimes ran ahead of the actual work — and

Edison found himself criticised in some quarters as a publicity-seeking showman who could not live up to his claims. As the year 1879 drew to its close, however, Edison was ready to confound the critics.

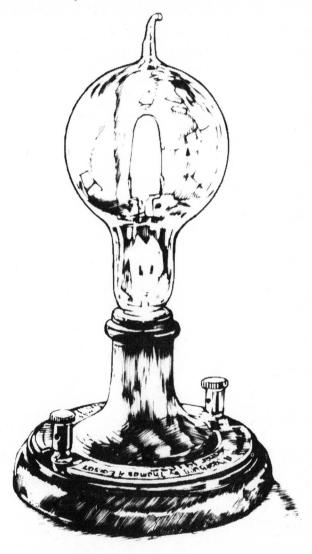

Edison's first incandescent lamp

Just after Christmas 1879 a small group of important visitors went out to Menlo Park, to see the new invention for themselves. One of them was the New York correspondent of the London *Times*. As he told his readers, he set off in a spirit of mild disbelief, aware that the public were beginning to question Edison's chances of 'ever accomplishing anything important in this field of experiment'. What he saw astounded him. Menlo Park was lit up by electric lighting. Indoors, people were able to read and work by the 'Edison lamp'; outside, as darkness fell, the street shone with the clear, attractive glow of electric lights. After 'Fifteen Months of Toil', as another newspaper put it, the lighting of the future had arrived.

The news of Edison's achievement flashed across the world. Once again he found himself hailed as a scientific genius and treated as an international celebrity. Once again, the crowds came pouring out to Menlo Park in their thousands, eager to see the wonder for themselves.

And once again, unfortunately, there were lawsuits to be fought. Though Edison had been the first inventor in America to produce a successful incandescent light bulb, in England Joseph Swan had achieved a similar breakthrough at about the same time. Edison had managed to patent his first, however, and with the power of a business organisation behind him, as well as his personal fame, he seemed set to take over the huge new market for electric lighting. Then Joseph Swan set up his own company, in competition, in 1880, and the disputes over rights and patents dragged on until, three years later, the inventors reached the most practical

Edison with the 'Edison effect lamp', an invention which
earned him the nickname 'the father of the electronics industry'

compromise, by joining forces to form one large company.

The creation of the incandescent light bulb was only the beginning of the story of electric lighting for all. Edison worked on, researching methods by which the electricity could be supplied, improving the light-bulb, trying out new and better materials for the filament. To make life easier at this busy time, he took on a secretary, a clever young Cockney named Samuel Insull. With Insull looking after his business affairs, Edison was free to carry on with what he liked best — inventing.

9 'Interests: Everything'

The inventions which made Thomas Edison's name a household word were almost all produced in just ten crowded years, while he was working at Menlo Park, from 1870 to 1880. Yet the fact that he had become a legend in his own lifetime before he was forty did nothing to lessen Edison's enthusiasm for new projects, or his capacity for sheer hard work. 'Interests: Everything', he once wrote in a visitors' book, when he was in his sixties, and the later years of his life were filled with ideas, inventions and activities of all kinds. Observers often remarked that the great Mr Edison liked nothing better than to roll up his shirt-sleeves and settle down at his work-bench, even when he was rich and famous.

At home, as well as in his working life, he faced changes and challenges. To his sorrow, his first wife died of typhoid fever at their Menlo Park house, in the summer of 1884. Edison was heartbroken; though she stayed very much in the background, Mary Edison had provided him with constant love and support, and in her own way she had contributed a great deal to his success.

The fact that their daughter and two sons were now

Edison with his second wife Mina

motherless may have prompted Edison to consider remarriage sooner than he would otherwise have done. At all events, he found himself falling in love again during the following year, and in the autumn of 1885 he proposed to the woman who was to be his second wife —

Mina Miller. Unlike Mary, the second Mrs Edison was a forceful character, and unlike Edison himself, she enjoyed fashion and society. Yet they were happy together, and three more children were born to them — Charles, Theodore and Madeleine. In many ways, Edison was a distant father, far more at home in the laboratory than the nursery, and he had some odd ideas as to what his children's interests, and even their toys, should be. Yet he also spent happy hours amusing them, romping boisterously and telling them jokes and stories, or drawing pictures for them. Even when he grew old, there was a boyish quality about the great inventor.

To accommodate his mushrooming business ventures and provide him with more spacious and up-to-date laboratory facilities, Edison built a new 'industrial works' in the beautiful setting of the Orange Valley, New Jersey, in the late 1880s. Not far away was the magnificent house, called Glenmont, which had become his home shortly before his second marriage. Sadly, the historic Menlo Park was allowed to fall into decay after the Wizard left to work his magic at Orange Valley.

Wearing a long, checked overall over his dark suit, Edison still acted as host to visitors to his place of work, as he had in the old days at Menlo Park — and he enjoyed receiving journalists more than ever. Whether he was researching the possibilities of an all-electric railway, or investing large amounts of time and money in iron-ore mining, or concrete construction, the newspapers were eager to report on every detail of Thomas Edison's current projects. As one of the earliest modern 'media figures', not only his actions but even his

Edison listening to a phonograph

thoughts were considered newsworthy; in regular yearly interviews on his birthday, he was asked for his opinion on every subject under the sun, from the education of children (he believed they should be more excitingly taught) to his opinion of God (he refused to accept that there was one.)

Probably the best-publicised of all Edison's inventions was his phonograph. As the 19th century progressed, he continued to develop and improve his famous 'baby', although he did his best to resist changing his original cylinders for the more modern flat discs, until well into the 20th century. The famous voices recorded on the phonograph included those of Queen Victoria, the poet

Edison operating a motion picture machine

Edison with Henry Ford and the electrically-powered Studebaker

Robert Browning — who forgot his lines half-way through reciting 'How They Brought the Good News from Ghent to Aix' — and the great German politician Count Bismarck, who foreshadowed the Watergate scandal by suggesting that such a machine might one day be used to record the secrets of political discussions.

Having given the world the means to record sound, Edison also played a part in the early stages of the film industry. His own inventions in this field were limited, and the early film projector known as the 'Edison Vitascope' was not, in fact, his creation. But his interest in the beginnings of the motion picture business encouraged others, and he became closely involved in the legal and commercial side of this new American industry. He even took part in developing another modern marvel — the motor-car. Henry Ford, inventor of the Ford automobile, had at one time been Edison's chief engineer, and as Ford carved out his own brilliant career, the two men remained close friends. Edison worked with Ford on plans for an electrically-powered car, before it became clear that petrol was to be the 20th-century motor fuel.

Strangely, one of Edison's most important discoveries was of no practical use to him. The so-called 'Edison effect', which he patented in 1883, concerned the movement of a 'force' or current inside a sealed glass bulb — the forerunner of the electron tube. It was to earn him the nickname of 'the father of the electronics industry' from later generations.

The boy who, in the 1860s, had sold newspapers during the American Civil War was an old man by 1917, when America entered the First World War. By nature Edison was a convinced pacifist, but he was willing to help his country's war-effort, and he applied his skills to devising naval weaponry. Where possible, he worked on devices that would be used for defence, or subsequent peacetime purposes, such as underwater telephone lines.

Both physically and mentally, Thomas Edison remained active until he was in his eighties — busying

Edison in old age

himself with schemes and inventions, enjoying the honours and accolades that were heaped upon him all over the world. In 1929, during a celebration banquet, organised by Henry Ford, to mark the 50th anniversary of the invention of the electric light bulb, Edison was struck down by an attack of Bright's disease. Bravely, he struggled for life for nearly two more years, but on 18 October 1931, the end came. America and the world mourned him as one of the great men of modern times.

On the evening of 21 October, all over the United States of America, the electric lights in homes and streets were turned out for one minute, in token of remembrance. Even the torch on the Statue of Liberty went dark. For Thomas Alva Edison, 'the man who invented the future', there could have been no more fitting tribute.

Important Events In The Life of Thomas Alva Edison
(1847 — 1931)

1855 — 8yrsold

1868	Patents his first real invention, an electrographic vote recorder
1869	Goes to New York, finds employment with Laws Gold Reporting Co., and produces his first commercially successful inventions
1871	Sets up his own 'invention factory' in Newark, New Jersey
1871, 25 December	Marries his first wife, Mary Stilwell
1876	Starts his laboratory and workshops at Menlo Park, New Jersey
1876	Invents his carbon button transmitter for use in the telephone receiver

1877, 4 December	The phonograph is demonstrated for the first time
1879	Produces the first successful incandescent light bulb in the USA
1885, 24 February	Marries his second wife, Mina Miller
1887	Sets up a new laboratory at West Orange, Orange Valley, New Jersey
1917-18	Conducts naval research for the First World War effort
1928	Awarded a gold medal by Congress, for producing inventions that 'revolutionised civilisation'